W9-AUI-525

Sailboat Lost

Leonard Everett Fisher

Macmillan Publishing Company   New York

Collier Macmillan Canada   Toronto

Maxwell Macmillan International Publishing Group

New York   Oxford   Singapore   Sydney

Macmillan Publishing Company, 866 Third Avenue, New York, NY 10022.
Collier Macmillan Canada, Inc., 1200 Eglinton Avenue East, Suite 200, Don Mills, Ontario M3C 3N1.

First edition   Printed in the United States of America   10   9   8   7   6   5   4   3   2   1

The text of this book is set in 16 point ITC Goudy Sans Medium Italic.
The illustrations are rendered in acrylic paints on paper.

Library of Congress Cataloging-in-Publication Data
Fisher, Leonard Everett.
Sailboat lost / Leonard Everett Fisher.—1st ed.   p.   cm.
Summary: Two boys are stranded when their boat is carried
away by a high tide and then rescued when it returns.
ISBN 0-02-735351-6
[1. Boats and boating—Fiction. 2. Stories in rhyme.] I. Title
PZ8.3.F635Sai   1991   [E]—dc20   90-21504

To the family sailors

They sailed to the secret shore
and beached their boat to explore.
But the tide rose high, their boat went free;
she left them stranded and turned to the sea.
Blown by the wind of a racing sail;
caught in the wake of another's trail;
a possible target for a submarine;
surrounded by sharks long and mean;
she found a fog in which to hide,
only to be trapped in a storm-tossed ride.
Adrift and lost in bright sunshine,
she let a gull take up her line.
Then friendly dolphins helped her reach
the soft damp sand of the breezy beach.
No longer marooned, they could explore
until they sailed from the secret shore.